                                              FADE IN:

EXT. BINGHAMTON, NEW YORK - DUSK

New Year's Eve, 1905.

Snow falls, as an icy Susquehanna River flows forcibly — to
WHITE.

EXT. KILMER MANSION - NIGHT

Bronze dragon sconces — breathing fire — guard the front of a
formidable Riverside Drive residence. A wrought-iron fence
flashes the letter "K" emblazoned atop.

INT. FOYER - NIGHT

Guests mingle and drink cocktails in grand parlors, alongside
a breathtaking rosewood staircase.

                    MR. DAVIDGE
              Land of opportunity. A valley of
              opportunity, right here in New
              York.

He turns to his wife:

                    MRS. DAVIDGE
              Rumor has it that the Robersons'
              ballroom is empty tonight—

                    MR. DAVIDGE
              Kilmer stole their guest list!

The smell of a feast and fireplaces fills the flush rooms of
this castle.

INT. PARLOR - NIGHT

Women in ruffled blouses and men in dinner jackets whisper
about the Kilmer empire.

                    MR. ROSE
              I hear the Kilmers are concerned
              about a bill coming in the
              legislature that will regulate
              patent medicine labels.

                    MRS. ROSE
          Can't we celebrate the coming of a
          new year without gossip?

Her husband takes a frustrated puff from a cigar.

INT. PARLOR - NIGHT

An august businessman, Jonas Kilmer, enters a boisterous
room:

                    JONAS
          *Indulge yourselves in food and
          drink!* My son — Willis Sharpe
          Kilmer — will be here shortly. He
          left New York City late — his best
          friend down there just got the damn
          mayoral election *stolen* from him!

Guests cry out, as Jonas exits.

                    MR. DAVIDGE
          Kilmers are also havin' frictions
          with that sanctimonious shoemaker
          who's expandin' in Lestershire.
          Valley may not be big enough for
          both—

                    MRS. DAVIDGE
          Apparently Binghamton wasn't.
          Darling, pour us more gin?

                                        DISSOLVE TO:

INT. KITCHEN - DAY

Port Crane, New York. Summer of 1868.

Pots boil vigorously on a wood-burning stove. A young woman
sits at a rickety table, chewing a cork like a squirrel. A
young man with a mutton-chops beard bursts in:

                    ANDRAL
          *Thousands have kidney trouble and
          don't know it!*

She stops, stunned. The young man — Sylvester Andral Kilmer —
is fresh from experimenting with concoctions and cures.

                    AURELIA
          Your corks will fit the bottles
          now.

Smiling, she presents a platter of chewed corks.

                                        DISSOLVE TO:

EXT. LACKAWANNA RAILROAD STATION - NIGHT

Binghamton is frigid and still as midnight approaches. A
porter pulls from a cigar and exhales.

EXT. LACKAWANNA RAILROAD STATION - CONTINUOUS

Snow falls on a downtown Delaware, Lackawanna & Western
terminal and its red brick bell tower. An oncoming train's
headlamp is visible in the distance.

EXT. TRAIN - NIGHT

The locomotive whistles, as a gleaming stone building emerges
beyond a railway platform.

EXT. LACKAWANNA RAILROAD STATION - NIGHT

The train rumbles into the station. The last railcar has
inscribed on its side: REMLIK.

EXT. PLATFORM - NIGHT

The porter readies the railcar's staircase; his breath
visible in brumal air. The door opens.

EXT. PLATFORM - CONTINUOUS

Willis Sharpe Kilmer — consummate rake, imposing and dressed
in a black topcoat and white fedora — steps out of his
private varnish and down the stairs.

He leans on a cane and flips a shiny coin to the porter.

                    PORTER
          Thank'ya, Mister Kilma'—

Willis motions toward the glistening stone building ahead,
and booms:

                    WILLIS
          I got six boxcars of Swamp-Root
          shipping out in the morning!

He walks off, toward a waiting carriage.

INT./EXT. DOWNTOWN BINGHAMTON - NIGHT

Willis's carriage clacks through snowy streets. He turns past
a pristine Beaux-Arts tower — the city's tallest building —
onto a teeming thoroughfare, as townspeople await the
midnight celebration.

                    WILLIS
               (to his driver)
          Whip anybody who gets in our way!

INT. KILMER MANSION - NIGHT

Guests gather in a grand room. In unison, they count down by
a grandfather clock and raging fireplace:

                    MALE GUEST
          Three!

                    FEMALE GUEST
          Two!

                    JONAS
          One!

They rejoice with calls of "happy new year" and toast with
white wine.

EXT. KILMER MANSION - NIGHT

Windows are illuminated, while snowflakes swirl as if in a
snow globe. Willis's carriage arrives.

INT. KILMER MANSION - NIGHT

Willis enters the ballroom:

                    WILLIS
          ...can't party without *me!*

Guests erupt into laughter as Willis's charisma beams through
the room. His father places a hand on Willis's shoulder,
welcoming him back.

                    WILLIS (CONT'D)
          Please, allow me to pour a drink—

He struts to the bar, slowly sliding a bottle across its
marble top: Swamp-Root Kidney, Liver & Bladder Cure. The
Great Specific. He mixes its blood-tinged tonic with ice and
a shot of bourbon.

                    WILLIS (CONT'D)
          I need to soothe my nerves from
          that trip.

He throws back the cocktail.

                    JONAS
          It remedies urinary trouble, fever,
          dropsy, and gout! To the house that
          Swamp-Root built—

Jonas takes a shot of whiskey.

                    MALE GUEST
               (under his breath)
          Bullshit snake oil. What's it *truly*
          good for?

                                        CUT TO BLACK.

EXT. HOSPITAL - MORNING

Spring, 1876.

A handsome brick building, upon which sunlight beams down.

INT. LAB - DAY

Sylvester Andral Kilmer, M.D. — with hallmark mutton chops,
and his title visible on the door — studies rows of jars on a
shelf. They are labeled by small paper slips: Uterine &
Ovarian Cure and Cough Cure Oil.

INT. EXAM ROOM #1 - DAY

Andral smiles at a patient.

                    ANDRAL
          What afflicts you today?

                    MALE PATIENT
          Pain pissing, and in my abdomen—

                    ANDRAL
          Do you know that thousands of
          people — *millions*, in fact — have
          kidney trouble. But don't know
          it...

The patient is silent.

                    ANDRAL (CONT'D)
          I'll write you a prescription for
          one of my proprietary herbal cures.

INT. HALLWAY - DAY

Andral knocks on the door of another room.

INT. EXAM ROOM #2 - DAY

Andral rubs his finger over a large, discolored mole. The
patient's face is stricken; her eyes do not blink.

                    ANDRAL
          This is carcinoma, a malignant skin
          disease — *cancer.*

The patient gasps.

                    ANDRAL (CONT'D)
          It is dangerous, but there's hope.
          I have been studying treatments
          since the tragic death of my
          father, Daniel Kilmer, from cancer.

                    FEMALE PATIENT
          What can be done?

                    ANDRAL
          I've developed numerous herbal
          cures, and a de-cancerizing removal
          system, since medical school. As
          well as a theory of cancer—

                    FEMALE PATIENT
          What are *those?*

Andral pauses.

                    ANDRAL
          The similarity of structure in
          plants and animals shows a common
          origin for all organic life.
                    (MORE)

                    ANDRAL (CONT'D)
          I am the first man to discover that
          fungus growths — *toadstools* — on
          stumps and trees are similar to
          cancer on the human body. That's
          what cancer is — an animalized
          toadstool.

                    FEMALE PATIENT
          I feel safer already.

                    ANDRAL
          Rest assured, the utter failures —
          caustics, burnings, plasters, the
          fatal knife — will be laid aside.
          Your cancer, this bestial fungus,
          will loosen its grasp and fall off
          your body like a scab!

The patient bursts into tears.

                    FEMALE PATIENT
          Oh thank you, doctor!

                    ANDRAL
          On my father's grave, I swore to
          become one thing: *cancer's
          conqueror.*

                                        CUT TO:

EXT. NEW YORK CITY - DAY

The swell of the East River swiftly carries chunks of ice, as
New York Harbor teems with boats.

EXT. BROOKLYN BRIDGE - DAY

Jonas Kilmer, a sharply dressed businessman in his early
thirties, takes in this vista from the Brooklyn Bridge
construction site. Children run past him, playing and
laughing. The city is young — majestic.

EXT. CITY HALL - DAY

Briskly, Jonas walks past City Hall on his way to work.

EXT. CHAMBERS STREET - DAY

He stares at a recently completed Tweed Courthouse; an
imposing Italianate palace built on corruption.

EXT. H.B. CLAFLIN & COMPANY - DAY

Jonas continues toward his employer, H.B. Claflin & Company, the world's largest wholesale dry-goods house. Broadway is gridlocked with horse-drawn drays, moving goods to and from Claflin's dominating presence along Worth Street.

INT. LAB - DAY

Andral pours potions from large jars into small vials. He adheres a printed label: Kidney Cure.

                    ANDRAL
          Please deliver this to the first
          exam room.

                    ASSISTANT
          Yes, Doctor!

                    ANDRAL
          It's astounding—

His assistant turns.

                    ANDRAL (CONT'D)
          Selling cures is bringing in more
          money than seeing patients.

INT. H.B. CLAFLIN & COMPANY - DAY

Claflin's cavernous interior is filled with flannels, shawls, hoods, scarves, and gloves. Men in identical black suits and bowler hats work intensely, as if inside of an anthill. Jonas enters:

                    CROSBY
          Jonas Kilmer!

                    JONAS
          How are you, Crosby?

                    CROSBY
          On the rise, my friend!

Jonas meanders through aisles of merchandise and a bustle of men shouting back and forth. He reaches a small wooden desk in the corner of an open floor plan, and looks at a paper schedule pinned to the wall.

                    JONAS
          The Ladies Mile. Lord & Taylor.
          Arnold Constable...

EXT. VIRGIL STREET, BINGHAMTON - DUSK

Andral dwells within a street-corner complex; his medical
office and nascent patent medicine business are attached to
his home. He turns a doorknob and enters.

                         ANDRAL
               Hattie?

His wife emerges from a side room.

                         HARRIET
               Hello, dear.

                         ANDRAL
               I'll see my brother Jonas tomorrow
               in New York City—

                         HARRIET
               Lovely!

She smiles.

                                             DISSOLVE TO:

INT./EXT. TRAIN - DAY

Andral looks out of a window; trees flicker past him as if in
a flip book. The train, swiftly and loudly, descends into a
dark, stone tunnel — to BLACK.

INT. LORD & TAYLOR - DAY

Jonas rides in an elevator with a department store purchasing
agent, who shows a gleaming smile.

                         AGENT
               Among the first of its kind: a
               steam-powered passenger elevator.

                         JONAS
               Amazing—

                         AGENT
               We're entering a new age — *an
               industrial revolution!*

The elevator doors open to a vibrant ground floor packed with
people and merchandise.

EXT. FERRY - DAY

Andral stares across the water from Jersey City to Lower Manhattan; dense buildings are visible from the ferry.

EXT. BROADWAY & 20TH STREET - DAY

The sun sets; streets fill with people. Hooves clatter as horse stench dominates Broadway. Jonas steps out of Lord & Taylor.

His black leather shoe submerges into a steamy pile:

                    JONAS
          ...shit!

Jonas shakes off horse droppings. He hands a coin to a street merchant for a bag of roasted chestnuts, then savors their faintly sweet and woody taste. His eyes close.

EXT. CORTLANDT STREET - DUSK

Andral's ferry arrives. He peers over a crowd. His austere black suit and mutton-chops beard look as if he is stepping out of wintry upstate church rather than onto the island of Manhattan.

                    JONAS
          Andral!

Jonas sees him in the crowd and approaches:

                    JONAS (CONT'D)
          Welcome! Welcome to the big town.
          It's lovely to see you—

Andral beams with satisfaction.

                    ANDRAL
          It is wonderful to see you as well,
          Jonas!

They shake hands and embrace.

EXT. BEAVER STREET - NIGHT

A heavy fog envelops Lower Manhattan.

EXT. DELMONICO'S - NIGHT

Beneath eerie gas lighting, Jonas and Andral enter thick wooden doors of Delmonico's, at the corner of Beaver and South William Streets.

INT. DELMONICO'S - NIGHT

                    HOST
          Gentlemen. How do you do?

                    JONAS
          Jonas M. Kilmer. I have a
          reservation for eight o'clock.

                    HOST
          Follow me this way.

INT. DELMONICO'S - CONTINUOUS

Jonas and Andral are seated; they receive menus and water with lemon slices.

                    JONAS
          An oyster plate—

                    WAITER
          Yes, sir.

                    JONAS
          With a glass of Zinfandel.

                    WAITER
          Of course.

The waiter exits.

                    ANDRAL
          I see that you've developed
          expensive tastes in New York!

                    JONAS
          You wouldn't believe the economic
          transformation—

                    ANDRAL
          How so?

Over a flickering candle, Jonas leans in:

> JONAS
> Despite 1873 — its stock market
> panic, a few years back — the
> fortunes are staggering.

> ANDRAL
> I see it in Binghamton as well; and
> with a boom in my medical business.
> But money isn't everything—

Jonas pauses for reflection.

> JONAS
> Of course. My son Willis is eight
> years old and doing well in school.
> He's a sharp young man—

> ANDRAL
> *Magnificent!*

EXT. SOUTH WILLIAM STREET - NIGHT

Fog creeps through narrow streets.

INT. DELMONICO'S - NIGHT

> JONAS
> What about your medical business,
> this boom that you speak of?

The waiter interrupts:

> WAITER
> May I take your orders, gentlemen?

> JONAS
> I'll have the Delmonico steak.

> WAITER
> With potatoes?

> JONAS
> Yes, please.

> WAITER
> For you, sir?

> ANDRAL
> I will start with clam chowder.
> Then the mallard duck.

                    WAITER
          And to drink?

                    ANDRAL
          Tea.

                    WAITER
          Thank you.

He collects their menus and walks away.

INT. DELMONICO'S - CONTINUOUS

                    JONAS
          Your medical business?

                    ANDRAL
          It is prospering—

                    JONAS
          Tell me!

                    ANDRAL
          My practice has patients all over
          the state. But I am obtaining more
          money from the preparation of
          cures—

                    JONAS
          What?

                    ANDRAL
          I can't believe it myself.

The waiter returns.

                    WAITER
          Your oysters, sir. And our house
          chowder—

                    ANDRAL
          Thank you.

                    WAITER
          Zinfandel—

                    JONAS
          Beautiful!

                    WAITER
          Gentlemen, enjoy.

Jonas, deeply intrigued, leans in toward Andral:

                    JONAS
          What are these cures?

Andral raises an eyebrow.

                    ANDRAL
          You won't believe my developments.

                    JONAS
          You can't be serious; is it
          millions?

                    ANDRAL
          Far, far bigger—

Jonas's eyes open wide.

                    ANDRAL (CONT'D)
          My progress toward a cancer cure.

Jonas is slack-jawed.

INT. DELMONICO'S - CONTINUOUS

                    ANDRAL
          Don't you find it odd that my clam
          chowder is red?

                    JONAS
          Manhattan-style.

                    ANDRAL
          Ah!

                    JONAS
          Why not expand the cures as a
          business?

                    ANDRAL
          I handle what I can.

                    JONAS
          There may be an opportunity; this
          could be our ticket—

Andral senses his disinterest in curing disease.

                    ANDRAL
          Our ticket to *what?*

Investment bankers gather at the bar; dressed in perfectly-
tailored suits; their hair combed back. Sweet cigar smoke
fills the room.

                    ANDRAL (CONT'D)
          Cures are only a supplement to my
          medical practice.

EXT. BEAVER STREET - NIGHT

Supernatural gas lighting sifts through dense fog. The street
is empty, as a black hansom cab led by a black horse appears.

INT. DELMONICO'S - NIGHT

Two men in impeccable black suits enter as, suddenly, the
room falls silent.

INT. DELMONICO'S - CONTINUOUS

The host is on edge, careful with his manners:

                    HOST
          Gentlemen, welcome!

He pauses with a warm smile.

                    HOST (CONT'D)
          We've been awaiting your arrival
          from the Buckingham Hotel. Please,
          follow me—

Bankers at the bar peer at the last man — pale, with a
meticulous mustache, a spectral presence — as he moves in
silence to his seat.

INT. DELMONICO'S - CONTINUOUS

Jonas observes this reaction and is mesmerized.

                    WAITER
          Sir, your Delmonico steak.

                    JONAS
          Wonderful—

                    WAITER
          And the mallard, for my gentleman
          to the left. Is there anything
          else?

                    JONAS
          May I ask—

He pauses.

                    JONAS (CONT'D)
          Who is that man that just walked
          in, commanding such a reaction?

The waiter freezes.

                    WAITER
          John D. Rockefeller, captain of
          industry; one of the richest men in
          America.

Jonas gazes.

                                        DISSOLVE TO:

EXT. BROAD STREET - NIGHT

The brothers cut through a cool night. Jonas hails a
carriage.

                    JONAS
          Grand Hotel, please. Broadway and
          Thirty-First!

He shuts a small door and the horse gallops off.

INT./EXT. WALL STREET - NIGHT

The brothers crane their bald heads to look at the New York
Stock Exchange.

                    ANDRAL
          What is that building?

                    JONAS
          The stock exchange, where ownership
          of mighty railroads changes hands!

Andral stares suspiciously.

INT./EXT. BROADWAY - NIGHT

The brothers' carriage turns past Trinity Church.

                    ANDRAL
          Stunning-

Its spire and gravestones rise out of the fog.

                    JONAS
          Remind you of home?

                    ANDRAL
          Much like Binghamton's First
          Presbyterian!

INT./EXT. BROADWAY - CONTINUOUS

They enter a canyon of office towers on Broadway.

                    JONAS
          I'd love to crack out on my own in
          business.

                    ANDRAL
          Risky for a man with a young
          family—

                    JONAS
          How do you reconcile that with your
          son, Ulysses?

                    ANDRAL
          I'm a doctor, not a businessman.

INT./EXT. BROADWAY - CONTINUOUS

Their carriage moves beneath monumental buildings.

                    JONAS
          I wonder if that oil man is
          shopping for a showpiece like
          these—

He waves a hand at the towers surrounding them.

                    ANDRAL
          Rockefeller? He's from Tioga
          County, next to Binghamton—

                    JONAS
          What?

                    ANDRAL
          Yes, I know of him. Maybe a year
          older than me. His family is known
          across the southern tier of New
          York.

INT. CARRIAGE - NIGHT

Jonas takes a pair of tickets from his jacket pocket.

                    JONAS
          "A Trip to the Moon"!

Andral laughs.

                    ANDRAL
          What is that?

                    JONAS
          A stage play, for which I have our
          tickets.

                    ANDRAL
          Tonight?

Jonas hands him a ticket.

                    JONAS
          On our way!

Their carriage canters through the night.

INT./EXT. BROADWAY & BROOME STREET - NIGHT

The brothers pass through an intersection, with cast-iron
buildings, illuminated by textile firms working at this late
hour.

                    ANDRAL
          Gorgeous architecture.

                    JONAS
          Prosperity, brother!

                    ANDRAL
          That one—

He points to E.V. Haughwout's building — a Renaissance
Revival — and its prefabricated colonnades.

                    ANDRAL (CONT'D)
          Reminds me of Isaac Perry's new
          office in Binghamton!

INT. CARRIAGE - NIGHT

Kilmers' cab slinks uptown; through a black Nile, teeming
with beasts and lizards.

                    JONAS
          You mentioned Rockefeller—

                    ANDRAL
          You're enamored with wealth.

                    JONAS
          I'm intrigued by his story—

Their faces are lit by gas lamps overhead.

                    ANDRAL
          His father is a botanic physician.

                    JONAS
          What specifically does he do?

                    ANDRAL
          Doc Rockefeller was originally in
          lumber, but began work on cancer
          cures, similar to my own.

Jonas smirks.

                    JONAS
          Why not think further on business
          expansion; it seems to have set a
          foundation for *his* son—

                    ANDRAL
          That was in decades past; the state
          of medicine has changed.

                    JONAS
          You don't think *they're* enamored by
          wealth?

Andral is angered.

                    ANDRAL
          There are higher callings—

                    JONAS
          Like what?

                    ANDRAL
          Like curing what killed *our* father!

INT./EXT. UNION SQUARE - NIGHT

The brothers' cab enters a lively expanse; Manhattan's
Rialto, with crowds lined up outside of theaters.

> JONAS
> How about practicality on this
> quest; don't you ask, what's it
> *truly good for?*

> ANDRAL
> I ask if you would rather tread an
> honorable path in Binghamton. *Or
> stumble to serve mammon in
> Manhattan!*

Jonas is taken aback by his rage.

INT./EXT. BROADWAY & 23RD STREET - NIGHT

As the brothers pass by Madison Square Park, Jonas strikes a
conciliatory tone:

> JONAS
> Andral, if you were to expand the
> medicine business, I would love to
> help.

> ANDRAL
> *What in the hell?*

They roll into Manhattan's vice district, with a sweet and
vile scent in the air.

> JONAS
> Reformers call this strip "Satan's
> Circus." Cops call it the
> Tenderloin. They get so many bribes
> that they aren't eating chuck steak
> anymore!

Women of the night walk the street alongside men in top hats.

> ANDRAL
> Never seen anything like it...

The brothers pass by saloon after saloon, sultry dance hall
after sultry dance hall.

EXT. BOOTH'S THEATRE - NIGHT

Jonas and Andral arrive at a granite Second Empire palace. A
line of people stretches around the block. The brothers exit
their carriage.

INT. BOOTH'S THEATRE - NIGHT

They enter a grand vestibule with Italian marble floors, an
imposing statue of Junius Brutus Booth, and frescoed
ceilings. Their tickets are taken.

INT. BOOTH'S THEATRE - NIGHT

Jonas and Andral take their seats beneath an elegant
chandelier.

                    JONAS
          Brother, I'm glad that you came.

Their eyes meet as the curtain rises.

                                        CUT TO BLACK.

                                        FADE IN:

EXT. PROSPECT PARK - DAWN

Trees shimmer in a reflection on Prospect Park Lake.

EXT. BROOKLYN BOROUGH HALL - DAY

Wind whips through fall foliage in downtown Brooklyn.

INT. SCHOOL - DAY

Willis, eight years old, sits in a classroom.

                    TEACHER
          Mister Gray?

A student looks up.

                    TEACHER (CONT'D)
          Your book report.

He rises to collect a graded paper.

                    TEACHER (CONT'D)
          Willis ... Sharpe ... Kilmer; here
          is yours—

Young Willis receives his paper.

                    TEACHER (CONT'D)
          Bold work.

EXT. SCHOOL - DAY

Still streets, as students shuffle out of school doors.

EXT. PARK - DAY

Children run around a playground.

                    RAWLINGS
          Horses!

He grabs Willis and points.

                    WILLIS
          Morgan stallions.

                    RAWLINGS
          Look at them muscles!

Bay horses' coats gleam as they pass.

                    WILLIS
          I hope we get a track like
          Saratoga, here in Brooklyn—

EXT. PARK - CONTINUOUS

The boys kick through a leaf pile.

                    RAWLINGS
          Willis!

                    WILLIS
          Let's ride our velocipedes to the
          Navy Yard.

They walk toward two unwieldy-yet-elegant Pickering & Davis
velocipedes.

                              DISSOLVE TO:

EXT. FIFTH AVENUE & 34TH STREET - DUSK

Jonas walks briskly.

                    JONAS
          I'm tired.

                    CROSBY
          Of what?

                    JONAS
          Of working for dry-goods houses;
          working for anybody else—

EXT. PARK - DUSK

Willis and Rawlings pass by a group of girls, including a
strikingly cute blonde.

EXT. FIFTH AVENUE & 34TH STREET - DUSK

                    CROSBY
          Why?

                    JONAS
          Why! Isn't it clear?

He stops and points at the late Alexander Turney Stewart's
lordly mansion:

                    JONAS (CONT'D)
          Does it look like we're on the
          right end of this deal?

EXT. PARK - DUSK

Willis and Rawlings are face to face with the girls.

                    ANNA
          Where are you going with those bone-
          shakers?

                    RAWLINGS
          To the Navy Yard!

Anna — a natural leader of her friends — is harsh despite her
young age.

                    WILLIS
          Where are you from?

                    ANNA
          Brooklyn Heights.

                    WILLIS
          Why not come with us? We'll see if
          there are ships being built—

She is silent, as her friends look to her.

                    ANNA
          Not today.

                    WILLIS
          Then hopefully another time!

He smiles.

                    ANNA
          What are those pants?

She points, as everyone looks at Willis; his eyes open wide
with insecurity.

                    WILLIS
          My pants?

                    ANNA
          They look so tight. Are you a girl,
          too?

They erupt into laughter, as Willis's cheeks turn red with
humiliation. He turns and rides away.

                                        DISSOLVE TO:

EXT. FIFTH AVENUE & 34TH STREET - NIGHT

Light beams down.

                    JONAS
          I want to move back upstate.

                    CROSBY
          Why?

                    JONAS
          Why, again, Crosby? Because I'm
          unhappy here. I feel stifled—

                    CROSBY
          But how so?

                    JONAS
          I'm not living up to my potential.

                    CROSBY
          What will you do upstate?

Their eyes meet, fearfully:

                    JONAS
          I don't know.

                                        DISSOLVE TO:

EXT. BROOKLYN - NIGHT

An elegant strip of brownstones is illuminated.

INT. HOME - NIGHT

Jonas and his wife clean up after dinner.

                    JONAS
          My brother and I had a beautiful
          time. You won't believe what Andral
          is doing—

                    JULIA
          Oh?

                    JONAS
          He has a booming business selling
          medicines.

                    JULIA
          Intriguing—

                    JONAS
          Julia, I have an important
          question.

He pauses, as she looks to him.

                    JONAS (CONT'D)
          What are your thoughts on moving
          back upstate?

She is surprised. Cautiously:

                    JULIA
          I would love to be closer to
          family.

                    JONAS
          We'll be closer to our relatives in
          Schoharie County, and Andral as
          well—

                    JULIA
          Wonderful!

                    JONAS
          Our time in Brooklyn has reached
          its end.

                    JULIA
          But what will you do?

He pauses.

                    JONAS
          I'll find a way to go into business
          for myself. We'll leave in the new
          year—

                    JULIA
          The only thing that I'll miss is
          Reverend Talmage's Tabernacle.

He smiles.

                    JONAS
          We'll make a new life for
          ourselves!

INT. ROOM - NIGHT

Jonas peeks into his son's bedroom:

                    JONAS
              (whispers)
          Willis?

                    WILLIS
          Yes, pop?

He looks up from a book on horses.

                    JONAS
          How would you feel about moving out
          of Brooklyn?

                    WILLIS
          To where, pop?

                    JONAS
          Upstate New York, where the rest of
          our family is.

                    WILLIS
          An adventure!

                    JONAS
          You wouldn't mind leaving school,
          and your friends?

                    WILLIS
          I don't know.

Jonas pauses, leaning toward him.

                    JONAS
          How do you feel?

                    WILLIS
          Afraid.

                    JONAS
          Of what, son?

                    WILLIS
          Of a new place.

                                        CUT TO BLACK.

EXT. WALL STREET, BINGHAMTON - MORNING

Andral walks along the Chenango River. He inhales deeply, as
a heavy smell of tobacco wafts down from nearby buildings. He
sneezes.

                    ANDRAL
          Tobacco?

EXT. CHENANGO RIVER - DAY

Andral examines a riverbank for nettles.

                    HULL
          Kilmer!

He looks up.

                    HULL (CONT'D)
          What are'ya doin' down there?

                    ANDRAL
          Searching for herbs!

                    HULL
          Come on up, and I'll treat'ya to
          lunch!

EXT. WALL STREET, BINGHAMTON - DAY

The two men walk along a promenade, beneath imposing new
factories.

> ANDRAL
> It smells like you're working with
> a potent leaf—

> HULL
> Ain't milkweed. That's Carolina's
> finest!

EXT. JOHN HULL JR. & CO. - DAY

Hull pulls open a door, beside which a sign displays his
company's name. The stench of tobacco strikes Andral's
olfactory system. He shuts his eyes.

> ANDRAL
> That is *not* milkweed.

> HULL
> Step inside, and I'll teach'ya
> about cigars—

INT. JOHN HULL JR. & CO. - DAY

They enter a room of long tables with dozens of men and women
working. Hull waves his arm:

> HULL
> Manufacturing!

The sweet scent of tobacco pervades the building.

> ANDRAL
> It's a stimulating leaf—

> HULL
> And a *profitable* one.

INT. JOHN HULL JR. & CO. - DAY

Hull unlocks the door to his office.

> HULL
> Bingham's agent, Joshua Whitney,
> brilliantly laid out our city—

They enter an austere room and take seats on opposite sides
of a desk.

                    HULL (CONT'D)
          Have a seat.

                    ANDRAL
          I've gone into business, myself—

                    HULL
          Oh!

                    ANDRAL
          Herbal remedies, a supplement to my
          medical practice.

Hull squints.

                    HULL
          Is that so?

                    ANDRAL
          It's coming along, but I need
          guidance.

                    HULL
          Roast chicken?

Andral is puzzled.

                    HULL (CONT'D)
          For lunch—

                    ANDRAL
          Please!

They smile.

                                        CUT TO:

EXT. NINTH AVENUE ELEVATED RAILWAY - DAY

Railcars screech across a curved track. Jonas turns sharply:

                    JONAS
          Excuse me?

                    MAN
          You too good!

                    JONAS
          What?

The sooty man, with his pants sagging and buttocks exposed, moves toward him and shouts:

                    MAN
          Think you too good!

Jonas recognizes him as mentally disturbed and quickly walks away.

                    JONAS
          Crazy.

                                             CUT TO:

INT. JOHN HULL JR. & CO. - DAY

Andral leans back and savors an apple.

                    ANDRAL
          You ship cigars by train?

                    HULL
          The rails are a godsend. I wouldn't
          have a business without them. New
          York can't run on canals and
          towpaths anymore — *I can't ship a*
          million cigars by mule!

                    ANDRAL
          How do you handle it all?

                    HULL
          Them people you seen workin'?
          That's immigrant labor. Irish, some
          Polish; gettin' others from Eastern
          Europe—

                                             CUT TO:

INT./EXT. - NINTH AVENUE ELEVATED RAILWAY - DAY

Jonas grasps an overhead pole in a train grinding down the track. It is packed with men in dark suits, heading downtown for work, and women exiting at busy Midtown stations for shopping.

INT./EXT. - NINTH AVENUE ELEVATED RAILWAY - CONTINUOUS

Jonas bumps into a financier, nattily dressed, who looks the same age.

                    JONAS
          Pardon me!

                    FINANCIER
          This city is going to hell.

Jonas responds smoothly:

                    JONAS
          Isn't it always?

                    FINANCIER
          You're here—

He scans Jonas from head to toe.

                    JONAS
          You're an investment banker?

                    FINANCIER
          I'm with Drexel Morgan.

Nearby, young men raise their eyebrows as they overhear,
visibly impressed. The train barrels through Manhattan.

                    JONAS
          What does it take to make it in
          business?

                    FINANCIER
          Brains — and balls.

Onlookers snicker. He raises his fist.

                    FINANCIER (CONT'D)
          Bullishness!

                    JONAS
          Bullishness?

                    FINANCIER
          Shrinking violets don't live like
          Vanderbilts.

INT./EXT. 34TH STREET STATION - DAY

Jonas steps out of a train car onto the platform at Ninth
Avenue. He moves swiftly toward the street.

EXT. 34TH STREET - DAY

Jonas weaves through a bustling block.

EXT. MANHATTAN MARKET - DAY

Jonas reaches Manhattan Market, a commercial palace of brick
and limestone at Eleventh Avenue; with vast arches and a cast-
iron spire, flying an American flag.

INT. MANHATTAN MARKET - CONTINUOUS

Jonas steps into this Taj Mahal of retail, struck by its
eldritch emptiness. He walks to a butcher's stall.

> JONAS
> Pound of strip steak.

> BUTCHER
> Coming right up!

The butcher whips out a cleaver.

> JONAS
> Why's this place quiet as a tomb?

> BUTCHER
> Tammany Hall.

They pause in silence.

> JONAS
> *Tammany Hall?*

> BUTCHER
> The city's political machine.

> JONAS
> What have they got to do with it?

The cleaver strikes.

> BUTCHER
> How's this look?

He holds up a slab of beef.

> JONAS
> Beautiful—

> BUTCHER
> Tammany controls Washington Market,
> and we were competition for them.
> They put us under with every weapon
> they could muster.

CUT TO:

INT. VIRGIL STREET, BINGHAMTON - DAY

Andral and Hull stroll through the former's primitive
workspace.

                    HULL
          First thing ya'need is an assembly
          line!

                    ANDRAL
          I'm a doctor, not a businessman.

                    HULL
          Andral, we'll model it after mine.

                    ANDRAL
          I shouldn't be traveling down this
          path—

They stop.

                    HULL
          Why's that?

                    ANDRAL
          Because I'm afraid that my work
          will be ridiculed.

                                        CUT TO:

INT. MANHATTAN MARKET - DAY

Jonas takes his beef wrapped in paper. Suddenly, he is jolted
by a stampede from behind.

                    JONAS
          What in the world is *that?*

                    BUTCHER
          Cattle, landing from barges at the
          dock. They're driven through a
          tunnel into our immense abattoir.

                    JONAS
          Abattoir?

                    BUTCHER
          Our slaughterhouse—

Jonas smirks.

INT. MANHATTAN MARKET - CONTINUOUS

A silhouette moves across the Market's long hall.

INT. MANHATTAN MARKET - DUSK

A gruff young man with a battered face appears behind Jonas.

                    MURPHY
          We got a new space open at
          Washington Market.

                    BUTCHER
          What'll it cost me?

The young man grins.

                    MURPHY
          Other than obedience to the
          Democratic Party?

Jonas turns toward him with a searing gaze.

                    MURPHY (CONT'D)
          One hundred and twenty a month.

                    JONAS
          Who do you think you are?

Silence.

                    MURPHY
          I'm with Tammany Hall.

They pause.

                    JONAS
          A thug dressed like a gentleman.

                    BUTCHER
          Stop this right now!

Murphy steps closer, face to face with Jonas.

                    MURPHY
          And you're nobody.

Spectators appear. Jonas is livid, his eyes ablaze. Suddenly,
Murphy spits in his face.

                    BUTCHER
          Stop this in my place of business!

Jonas, enraged, shoves Murphy — who then strikes Jonas's face.

                    BUTCHER (CONT'D)
          Stop!

Murphy spits again.

                    MURPHY
          (to Jonas)
          You're nobody.

Bystanders watch, as Jonas's mouth trickles blood.

                              FADE TO BLACK.

INT. VIRGIL STREET - MORNING

Easter, 1878.

Andral's shrieking son, aged three, runs to a boiling pot of eggs.

                    ULYSSES
          Time to paint them!

                    HARRIET
          Careful, Ulysses, they need to cool
          first—

His mother sets the pot on a table.

                    ANDRAL
          Can you name these colors, son?

Andral displays colorings to paint eggs with.

                    ULYSSES
          Blue?

                    ANDRAL
          Yes! That one is like a robin's
          egg, and here's lilac—

Calmly:

                    ANDRAL (CONT'D)
          What does this remind you of?

He points to yellow.

                    ULYSSES
          I don't know—

                    ANDRAL
          How about dandelions, or a baby
          chicken?

                    ULYSSES
          Yes!

Andral smiles and gives him a paint brush.

                                        DISSOLVE TO:

INT. HOME - DAY

Jonas looks into a mirror.

                    JONAS
          If I had a name like Rockefeller—

He examines a swollen lip.

                    JONAS (CONT'D)
          This won't happen again. *I'm done!*

He peers into his own eyes.

                    JONAS (CONT'D)
          I'm done runnin' around for scraps.
          I'm done feeling small—

                                        CUT TO:

INT. VIRGIL STREET - DAY

Andral pinches an egg with tongs.

                    ANDRAL
          Watch this!

He roasts its shell over a candle's flame, turning the egg
black.

                    ANDRAL (CONT'D)
          Examine this sooty shell.

He displays it to his son.

                    ANDRAL (CONT'D)
          And now, *behold—*

He drops the egg into a glass of water; and then, mystically,
holds it up.

                    ANDRAL (CONT'D)
          It has turned silver!

The submerged egg shimmers like mercury glass.

                                        DISSOLVE TO:

INT. - HOME - DAY

Jonas, shirtless, turns away from the mirror and shouts:

                    JONAS
          I'm done!

He picks up books and throws them onto his bed.

                    JONAS (CONT'D)
          Bring these. I'm done with New York
          City—

He turns back to the mirror and buttons up a white dress
shirt.

                    JONAS (CONT'D)
          Willis won't need to put up with
          what I have. That's a promise.

                                        CUT TO:

INT. VIRGIL STREET - DAY

Andral leans over his son's shoulder:

                    ANDRAL
          After you begin school, we'll try
          another experiment; creating a
          volcano from baking soda and
          vinegar.

                    ULYSSES
          Yes, papa!

                    ANDRAL
          Say after me, S-C-I-E-N-C-E.
          Science!

                    ULYSSES
          S-C-I-E-N-C-E—

                    ANDRAL
          Ulysses, one day you can become a
          doctor, too!

                    ULYSSES
          Can I see the flame?

Andral smiles and waves the candle.

                    ANDRAL
          How's this—

                    ULYSSES
          Wow!

Ulysses is mesmerized by fire.

                    ANDRAL
          Let's try another, demonstrating
          the food of life, called *oxygen—*

Andral sets a matchbook on the table; he pokes a match
through it, standing upright. He leans another match against
that, and lights its middle on fire.

                    ANDRAL (CONT'D)
          Watch!

The tilted match begins levitating, as their heads stay stuck
and blaze.

                    ANDRAL (CONT'D)
          Oxygen is being consumed from the
          air.

                    ULYSSES
          Oh—

                    ANDRAL
          And look!

Andral takes a glass and sets it upside down on the burning
matches, extinguishing them.

                    ULYSSES
          No!

                    ANDRAL
          Why did that happen, son?

Ulysses is silent.

                    ANDRAL (CONT'D)
          Because oxygen was cut off.

Harriet appears from behind.

                    HARRIET
          Boys, Easter ham is served!

                                        DISSOLVE TO:

EXT. DR. KILMER & CO. - DAY

Construction workers on scaffolding swiftly erect a building
at Chenango and Virgil Streets. Andral — standing at the
corner below, looking doubtful — turns to Hull:

                    ANDRAL
          You're sure about this?

Hull winks.

EXT. DR. KILMER & CO. - CONTINUOUS

A worker affixes lettering on the building: Dr. Kilmer's.

INT. DR. KILMER & CO. - CONTINUOUS

Young men set up a dispensary.

INT. DR. KILMER & CO. - CONTINUOUS

Andral stirs a vat.

INT. DR. KILMER & CO. - CONTINUOUS

Workers package a first run of bottles.

INT. DR. KILMER & CO. - DUSK

Hull and Andral stand in an office.

                    ANDRAL
          Good day!

                    HULL
          I'm prouda'ya, my friend.

Hull lights a cigar.

                    ANDRAL
          What about distribution, far beyond
          Binghamton?

                    HULL
          Stores.

                    ANDRAL
          Stores?

                    HULL
          Ya'need to sell your bottles like I
          sell my cigars — by rail and in
          stores!

                    ANDRAL
          But how?

Hull blows a ring of smoke.

                    HULL
          One step at a time.

                                        DISSOLVE TO:

INT. DR. KILMER & CO. - NIGHT

Andral — sitting in his office, alone — scans a newspaper
headline: FREIGHT BACK ON TRACK.

                    ANDRAL
          ...after last year's Great Railroad
          Strike?

He observes photographs of rolling stock and buildings
engulfed in flames.

                                        MATCH CUT TO:

EXT. LEBANON VALLEY RAILROAD BRIDGE - NIGHT

An inferno rages above the Schuylkill River.

                                        CUT TO:

INT. DR. KILMER & CO. - NIGHT

Andral shudders.

                    ANDRAL
          Nightmare.

He sighs:

                    ANDRAL (CONT'D)
          I don't know about all this...

                                        CUT TO BLACK.

EXT. SALINA STREET, SYRACUSE - MORNING

Summer sun on a thronging thoroughfare.

INT. GLOBE HOTEL, SYRACUSE - DAY

Andral peers through a contraption, examining a man's mouth.

                    ANDRAL
          You chew tobacco?

                    PATIENT
          How'd you know?

                    ANDRAL
          There is a white patch on the
          inside of your cheek — perhaps
          cancer.

                    PATIENT
          What?

                    ANDRAL
          I often observe cancer forming in
          areas of abrasion, chemical
          buildup, or previous injury.

                    PATIENT
          I don't want to die—

                    ANDRAL
          Then stop chewing tobacco right
          away, and I will monitor the inside
          of your mouth.

                    PATIENT
          I'll smoke instead—

Andral nods.

                    ANDRAL
          Fear not, as I shall offer you the
          most important message that has
          been transmitted to mankind in
          eighteen centuries: *cancer can be
          cured!*

The patient falls to his knees and holds Andral's ankles,
sobbing:

                    PATIENT
          Thank you, Doctor Kilmer.

                                        DISSOLVE TO:

EXT. TRAIN STATION - DAY

A locomotive steams into a staid station.

EXT. TRAIN STATION - CONTINUOUS

Jonas steps out, surveying his environs.

                    JONAS
          So this is Binghamton?

His wife and Willis, holding hands, are close behind. They
observe men working around a train depot.

                    JULIA
          It's cleaner than Brooklyn.

EXT. LEWIS STREET - DAY

The family walks to the corner of Lewis and Chenango Streets.
Jonas inhales deeply, taking in upstate's pristine air.

                    JONAS
          This is your new city, son. This
          city will be yours—

He puts a hand on Willis's shoulder.

EXT. VIRGIL STREET - DAY

Jonas knocks on Andral's door. It opens:

                    ANDRAL
          Jonas!

They embrace.

                    JONAS
          We meet again. I love you, brother—

                    ANDRAL
          I'm surprised to see you! And young
          Willis—

Andral pats Willis on the cheek.

                    ANDRAL (CONT'D)
          Come inside!

INT. VIRGIL STREET - CONTINUOUS

They traverse Andral's living room with curtains drawn.

                    ANDRAL
          Have a seat, and I'll bring water
          for everyone—

Jonas and his family relax on a sofa, as Ulysses runs into
the room.

                    JONAS
          Willis, say hello to your little
          cousin, *Ula*—

Willis tickles Ulysses' fleshy jowls.

INT. VIRGIL STREET - CONTINUOUS

Jonas sips from a glass of water.

                    ANDRAL
          I'm stunned that you are in
          Binghamton!

                    JONAS
          And I'm impressed with all that you
          have developed on this block—

Jonas motions toward the new dispensary and production space
next door.

                    JONAS (CONT'D)
          You've even got your name on a
          building!

Andral laughs.

INT. DR. KILMER & CO. - DAY

The brothers tour Andral's facility.

INT. DR. KILMER & CO. - CONTINUOUS

Andral points at a conical fermenter:

                    ANDRAL
          ...and this is a brewing vessel for
          buchu leaves.

                    JONAS
          Buchu leaves?

                    ANDRAL
          An herb that I import to make my
          best remedy: Swamp-Root!

                    JONAS
          What is *that?*

                    ANDRAL
          Swamp-Root is a tonic, blended with
          oil of juniper, skullcap, rhubarb
          root and, of course, swamp
          sassafras.

                    JONAS
          What does it do?

                    ANDRAL
          Its curative properties are *vast*:
          cleansing of the kidneys, catarrh
          of the bladder; it remedies
          rheumatism, Bright's disease,
          diabetes—

                    JONAS
          And more?

Andral grins.

                    ANDRAL
          And more! My business is founded on
          the true theory that God has
          provided in nature a remedy for
          every disease. Of tens of thousands
          of potential plants for medicine,
          only a few are known. Why stop
          short of what God permits for
          healing the sick?

INT. DR. KILMER & CO. - DAY

The brothers take seats in Andral's office.

                    JONAS
          I don't know what I'm going to do
          in Binghamton—

                    ANDRAL
          Perhaps a picnic at Ross Park,
          where there are animals to observe?

                    JONAS
          No, not leisure. To make a living—

                    ANDRAL
          Make a living?

                    JONAS
          I don't plan on returning to New
          York City.

                    ANDRAL
          You can't be serious?

                    JONAS
          I'm serious as cancer—

Andral raises his eyebrows.

                    ANDRAL
          You've come to join the mission?

Jonas thinks for a moment.

                    JONAS
          I have, brother—

                    ANDRAL
          The conquering of disease?

                    JONAS
          Yes, sir.

Andral is enraptured.

                    ANDRAL
          *For the benefit of suffering
          humanity?*

                    JONAS
          Absolutely—

                    ANDRAL
          We begin tomorrow!

Andral hugs him.

EXT. DR. KILMER & CO. - DAY

Jonas exits the building alone:

                    JONAS
          Well, at least I got a job.

He walks down the street as the sun sets.

                              DISSOLVE TO:

EXT. DR. KILMER & CO. - MORNING

Workers walk down Chenango Street and into Andral's facility.

INT. DR. KILMER & CO. - DAY

A supervisor places a crate of empty bottles at the beginning
of an assembly line.

                    EASLEY
          Let's fire it up!

Everything jolts into motion.

EXT. VIRGIL STREET - DAY

Willis and Ulysses play with toys in the yard.

                    WILLIS
          Ula, can you beat me?

Willis advances a wooden palomino horse to an imaginary
starting gate.

                    WILLIS (CONT'D)
          Let's race!

The boys, seven years apart, size each other up. Willis plays
an imaginary bugle.

                    WILLIS (CONT'D)
          Ready, go—

They sprint on all fours, pushing their wooden horses across
the lawn.

INT. DR. KILMER & CO. - DAY

Andral stands in a laboratory, surrounded by beakers, vials,
tubes, and flasks. He works feverishly.

                    EASLEY
          Doctor Kilmer—

Andral turns.

                    EASLEY (CONT'D)
          When we're fermenting, shall we
          extend it for one more day?

                    ANDRAL
          Yes, a longer fermentation will
          produce more alcohol, providing
          patients with greater relief.

Easley nods in confirmation.

                    ANDRAL (CONT'D)
          My motto is *"be always sure you're
          right, then go ahead"*! Let us
          follow that for our process—

EXT. VIRGIL STREET - DAY

Crossing an imaginary finish line, Willis throws up his arms:

                    WILLIS
          I am the trophy winner!

Ulysses, well behind, glares at him. Willis runs up and slaps
his cheek.

INT. DR. KILMER & CO. - DAY

Jonas holds up a consignment agreement.

                    JONAS
          Brother, I closed a deal with a
          pharmacy.

                    ANDRAL
          Spectacular!

                    JONAS
          Apparently I developed a little
          skill in New York City—

                    ANDRAL
          I couldn't be more grateful for our
          partnership. Jonas, we have
          everything to be proud of.

Andral lovingly embraces his brother.

INT. DR. KILMER & CO. - DUSK

Swamp-Root boxes are stacked at the end of an assembly line,
ready to be shipped.

                                        DISSOLVE TO:

EXT. BINGHAMTON HIGH SCHOOL - MORNING

Spring, 1886.

A red brick Victorian building by Isaac Perry; its dignity
evokes Cornell University's White Hall.

INT. BINGHAMTON HIGH SCHOOL - DAY

Willis runs down wooden stairs, sliding off a railing at
their end.

                    BENNETT
          Willis! You coming to the party
          tonight?

                    WILLIS
          Where is it?

                    BENNETT
          By the river—

                    WILLIS
          Will there be girls?

He grins.

                                        DISSOLVE TO:

EXT. SUSQUEHANNA RIVER - DUSK

A fire rages at the riverbank. A dapper young man taps a
wooden beer barrel.

                    BENNETT
          Line up with your cups!

A crowd of high school students awaits its alcohol.

EXT. SUSQUEHANNA RIVER - NIGHT

Willis sits on a stump and drinks beer.

> JARVIS
> What do you plan to do after high
> school?

> WILLIS
> I need to convince my old man to
> send me to college.

Fire flickers.

> JARVIS
> Isn't it too late?

> WILLIS
> I need to press my case.

Tall trees loom and host a symphony of insects.

> JARVIS
> What's your goal?

> WILLIS
> To ingratiate myself with those
> ladies over there—

Jarvis chuckles.

> JARVIS
> I mean in life.

> WILLIS
> More than hawking medical cures
> like my old man. He works
> constantly, and has no time to
> enjoy himself—

The girls come closer.

> WILLIS (CONT'D)
> *I want to live large.*

> JARVIS
> Elizabeth—

He calls out to one of the girls.

                    JARVIS (CONT'D)
          Come join us!

EXT. SUSQUEHANNA RIVER - CONTINUOUS

They sit on stumps and logs; their faces lit by a crackling
fire.

                    WILLIS
          Would you like another beer?

                    MARY
          Thanks—

Willis hands her a cup, and puffs from a cigar.

                    WILLIS
          I love the water.

                    ELIZABETH
          Water?

                    WILLIS
          Being by the river. Or lakes. Or
          the sea—

Moonlight reflects off a slow Susquehanna.

                    WILLIS (CONT'D)
          It's like we learn in school; the
          Euphrates, the Tigris, the Yellow
          River. The sustenance of
          civilization. That's what we have
          here, with the flourishing of
          industry in New York.

                    MARY
          It sounds like you paid more
          attention in class than we did.

Willis smiles.

EXT. SUSQUEHANNA RIVER - NIGHT

Willis and Mary are alone.

                    WILLIS
          I'm ready to get out in the world.

                    MARY
          To go where?

                    WILLIS
          I want to travel like a gentleman,
          like they do in Europe—

She speaks softly, as Willis moves closer:

                    MARY
          Romantic.

                    WILLIS
          To sail on a yacht—

He tucks his nose into the side of her neck, and begins
kissing.

                                        FADE TO BLACK.

EXT. DOWNTOWN BINGHAMTON - MORNING

Citizens hurry to work.

EXT. LESTER BROTHERS & CO. - DAY

A sizable factory sits at the corner of Washington and Henry
Streets.

INT. DR. KILMER & CO. - DAY

Bottles are filled on an assembly line.

INT. LESTER BROTHERS & CO. - DAY

Dozens of workers vigorously manufacture boots and shoes.

EXT. DR. KILMER & CO. - DAY

Boxes of Swamp-Root are loaded onto wagons.

INT. HOME - DUSK

Jonas pushes open the front door.

                    WILLIS
          Dad, how was your day?

Jonas tosses his tie onto a chair.

                    JONAS
          Long, tiring—

                    WILLIS
          But business is good?

Jonas sighs.

                    JONAS
          We have a long way to go, but one
          day it will all be yours—

                    WILLIS
          I was thinking—

He pauses.

                    JONAS
          Yes?

                    WILLIS
          I need more education.

                    JONAS
          And why is that?

                    WILLIS
          Because I can't manage the family
          business otherwise. I won't be able
          to navigate this world.

                    JONAS
          Why don't you apprentice at the
          company right away?

                    WILLIS
          Because it won't be good enough.
          Just look at all the gentlemen,
          back in New York City—

Jonas leans back and reflects.

                    JONAS
          If they're not college men, then
          their sons are. I understand what
          you're saying.

                    WILLIS
          So let me get more education, Dad,
          and we'll become like them. I will
          make us rich!

                                        DISSOLVE TO:

EXT. LIBE SLOPE, CORNELL UNIVERSITY - DAY

Willis gazes at Cayuga's idyllic curve, as chimes ring out in
the distance.

EXT. QUAD - DAY

Willis walks across a quadrangle, examining his surroundings.

                    WILLIS
          I can get used to this—

INT. ADMISSIONS OFFICE - DAY

A woman sits at a wooden desk, as Willis enters:

                    WILLIS
          I'm here to enroll in classes.

EXT. STONE STEPS - NIGHT

Under a full moon, Willis swills whiskey.

                    WILLIS
          So where'd you grow up?

                    BLAUVELT
          Rockland County, above the city—

                    WILLIS
          I lived in Brooklyn, but we moved
          up here to the woods!

Blauvelt laughs.

                    BLAUVELT
          Why'd you decide on Cornell?

                    WILLIS
          Close to home. I'm not sure if I
          would be comfortable in many other
          places—

                    BLAUVELT
          Do you want to go back downstate?

Willis pulls from a cigar.

                    WILLIS
          I want that social scene—

                    BLAUVELT
          You have a taste of it here.

                     WILLIS
          Girls, lifestyle. I want action—

A policeman surprises them from behind:

                    OFFICER
          Boys, no drinking on these steps!

EXT. WHITE HALL - MORNING

Fall foliage flares in front of a stone row.

INT. CLASSROOM - DAY

A professor walks in.

                   PROFESSOR
          Class, professor Henry Carter Adams
          will no longer teach this course. I
          am your new professor of economics.

                    STUDENT
          Was professor Adams dismissed
          because of his remarks supporting
          labor in Jay Gould's railroad
          strike?

                   PROFESSOR
          Ahem! Young man, our administration
          supports freedom of speech and is
          neutral on content. Let us begin
          today's class—

The student scoffs. Willis is seated in the front row.

                PROFESSOR (CONT'D)
          Advertising! A prominent role in
          today's economy. Why is it
          important?

Willis raises his hand.

                PROFESSOR (CONT'D)
          Yes?

                    WILLIS
          Because advertising increases
          potential demand?

                    PROFESSOR
          Exactly. When more people know
          about your product, its market size
          is that much larger.

INT. DR. KILMER & CO. - DAY

Jonas sits at a desk and signs papers. Andral enters.

                    JONAS
          We need help!

                    ANDRAL
          Hire as you wish. I'll be touring
          the state to see patients—

                    JONAS
          I'm interviewing a promising young
          man named Jerome Hadsell. I hope
          that he can assist us.

                    ANDRAL
          I am the doctor and you're the
          businessman — whatever judgment you
          think is best.

INT. DR. KILMER & CO. - DAY

A knocking at the door.

                    JONAS
          Come in!

                    HADSELL
          Hello, sir—

A man in his early twenties enters.

                    JONAS
          Take a seat. I'll cut right to it:
          we need help in our bustling
          business.

                    HADSELL
          I'm at your service, Mister Kilmer.

                    JONAS
          Look around. You'd feel competent
          in this environment?

                    HADSELL
          Indeed.

                    JONAS
          When can you begin?

                    HADSELL
          Tomorrow?

                    JONAS
          Report here at nine, not a minute
          late. You're originally from
          Schoharie County as well?

                    HADSELL
          Warnerville, sir.

                    JONAS
          We grew up in Cobleskill. Welcome
          to the family!

                                        DISSOLVE TO:

EXT. TRAIN - DAY

A passenger train cruises through the countryside.

INT. TRAIN - DAY

Willis reads the Ithaca Journal newspaper.

INT. HOME - DUSK

Willis pushes open the front door.

                    JONAS
          You're back!

                    WILLIS
          It was an intense semester—

Jonas smiles.

                    JONAS
          You'll have plenty of time to rest.

INT. HOME - CONTINUOUS

                    WILLIS
          Dad, I'm ready to join the company.

Jonas freezes.

                    JONAS
          What? What about college?

                    WILLIS
          I feel ready to work.

                    JONAS
          You want to drop out?

                    WILLIS
          I do.

Jonas pauses.

                    JONAS
          I want you to take over the
          company. For our legacy—

                    WILLIS
          If I follow you correctly.

                    JONAS
          Son, I couldn't be happier to have
          you back.

They embrace.

INT. DR. KILMER & CO. - DAY

Jonas leads a tour for Hadsell.

                    JONAS
          And here's our bottling area—

He motions toward a display of finished products.

                    JONAS (CONT'D)
          With our full line of family
          medicines — Autumn-Leaf Extract,
          Prompt Parilla Pills, Swamp-Root —
          our best seller, *a miracle cure!* —
          Female Remedy, Indian Consumption
          Oil; we've got U&O Meadow Plant
          Anointment — *another winner* — and
          Ocean-Weed Heart Remedy.

                    HADSELL
          Very impressive, sir.

                    JONAS
          Try a swig of Swamp-Root—

Jonas opens a bottle and hands it to Hadsell, who takes a
sip. His lips pucker:

>   HADSELL
>   Like an herbal wine!

>   JONAS
>   *With just as much alcohol.* My
>   brother brilliantly created our
>   products—

EXT. COMMERCIAL AVENUE - DAY

Jonas meets Willis on the street.

>   JONAS
>   Look at this dashing young man!

>   WILLIS
>   Hey, Dad—

>   JONAS
>   Ready for your first day?

>   WILLIS
>   The first day of my future.

Jonas grabs his shoulders:

>   JONAS
>   Exactly what I want to hear, son. I
>   couldn't be more proud of you.

>   WILLIS
>   What's this busy place?

He points at a makeshift factory next to a grist mill.

>   JONAS
>   Bundy Manufacturing. Run by a kooky
>   inventor, making clocks. But
>   they're growing like *wildfire*—

>   WILLIS
>   Sounds like uncle Andral!

Jonas smirks.

INT. DR. KILMER & CO. - DAY

Father and son walk into a meeting with Hadsell and Andral.

                    JONAS
          Gentlemen, we have a new team
          member—

Jonas smiles at Willis, as the others look on.

                    JONAS (CONT'D)
          In our family business!

                    ANDRAL
          What are we discussing today?

                    JONAS
          Advertising.

                    ANDRAL
          As you ask, what's it *truly* good
          for?

Jonas sharpens his gaze.

                    JONAS
          Willis made a point that people
          won't know about our products
          unless we advertise more.

                    ANDRAL
          What do you suggest?

Jonas looks to Willis.

                    WILLIS
          Signs, trade cards, maybe a "Guide
          to Health"—

                    ANDRAL
          A Guide to Health?

                    WILLIS
          A collection of testimonials. Your
          credentials. Images, information.
          And *sheet music*—

Willis smiles.

                    ANDRAL
          Sheet music? Isn't that a departure
          from curing invalids?

                    WILLIS
          We will exalt you as The Invalids'
          Benefactor.

                    ANDRAL
          That I am, young man.

Jonas stares blankly at Andral.

                                        DISSOLVE TO:

INT. CONSULTING ROOM - DAY

Andral enters to meet with a patient.

                    ANDRAL
          Have you been taking Swamp-Root as
          prescribed?

                    PATIENT
          I have—

                    ANDRAL
          And how is your kidney trouble?

                    PATIENT
          All gone now.

                    ANDRAL
          Miraculous!

                    PATIENT
          I was told by a dozen doctors that
          I'd never be relieved. That I was
          not long for this world. But Swamp-
          Root saved me—

Andral pauses for earnest reflection.

                    ANDRAL
          Doctor Edward Jenner died in 1823,
          but his discovery of vaccination
          still exists throughout the
          civilized world. William T. G.
          Morton has passed, yet lives on
          through his discovery of
          anesthesia. And long after Doctor
          Kilmer has left this earth, my name
          will be enshrined as the *discoverer
          of Swamp-Root*, the greatest cure of
          this century!

INT. HALLWAY - DAY

Jonas coldly listens on the other side of the door.

EXT. MAILBOX - DAY

A green letter from Dr. Kilmer & Co., featuring Andral's bust. "Sole Proprietors & Manufacturers." "Specific Family Medicines." "Take It Thyself!"

EXT. NEWSPAPER STAND - DAY

A printed advertisement: "Swamp-Root Cured Me." Followed by a testimonial from a Mrs. Miller: "I was raised from the dead!"

INT. DRUGSTORE - DAY

A compendium: "Guide to Health." Its cover has a drawing of Andral at his desk, seated among books and papers: "The Physician at Work." "BEWARE OF FRAUD AND IMPOSTERS!"

INT. DR. KILMER & CO. - DUSK

Rain patters on the roof, as Jonas enters Andral's office.

                    JONAS
          You have a moment?

                    ANDRAL
          What can I help you with?

                    JONAS
          I want to buy you out.

Andral is taken aback.

                    ANDRAL
          Excuse me?

                    JONAS
          Your share in the business.

                    ANDRAL
          You can't be serious. Why?

                    JONAS
          Because it will allow you to focus
          on your medical practice.

Andral thinks for a moment.

                    ANDRAL
          ...which is what I want.

                    JONAS
          Name your price.

                    ANDRAL
          You're sure about this?

                    JONAS
          As you say, you're the doctor, and
          I'm the businessman.

                    ANDRAL
          That's right. I don't want to be in
          manufacturing and marketing. I'm
          comfortable stepping aside—

                    JONAS
          Forty thousand dollars.

                    ANDRAL
          What?

                    JONAS
          Too low?

                    ANDRAL
          Far too high—

                    JONAS
          A fair price then. Forty thousand
          it is.

                              FADE TO BLACK.

EXT. MAIN STREET - MORNING

Leaden clouds loom over Binghamton, and horses trudge through
March sleet.

EXT. MAIN STREET - CONTINUOUS

Jonas and Willis ride in a carriage.

                    JONAS
          The business is ours.

                    WILLIS
          Huh?

                    JONAS
          I purchased your uncle Andral's
          stake, and now own a hundred
          percent.

                    WILLIS
          Really?

                    JONAS
          I did it for you. For us. This is
          our legacy. Your legacy.

                    WILLIS
          What do we know about discovering
          medicines?

                    JONAS
          We don't need to know.

                    WILLIS
          What do you mean?

                    JONAS
          Our product line is complete. We're
          not in the business of finding
          cures. We're in the business of
          selling them.

EXT. BEVIER STREET - DAY

A perch overlooking the glorious river valley.

EXT. FREDERICK STREET - DAY

Ulysses, eighteen years old, lights a cigarette. He gazes at
a flaring match and flicks it into a puddle.

EXT. CREEK - DAY

Andral examines a glass of water and inhales deeply:

                    ANDRAL
          Sulphur?

INT. OFFICE - DAY

Jonas pores over accounting.

INT. OFFICE - CONTINUOUS

Willis enters.

                    JONAS
          We're not in the fighting shape
          that I had thought.

                    WILLIS
          How so?

                    JONAS
          I was focused on sales, not the
          costs of your uncle's science
          experiments.

                    WILLIS
          What does that mean?

                    JONAS
          It means that we need to cut costs
          and sell more, or we're careening
          toward trouble—

                    WILLIS
          Right out of the gate?

Jonas loses his temper.

                    JONAS
          Get out and sell more!

INT. KITCHEN - DAY

                    ANDRAL
          Ulysses, come quick!

                    ULYSSES
          Yes, pop?

                    ANDRAL
          Smell this—

He holds up a glass of water.

                    ULYSSES
          —'uck, *rotten eggs!*

                    ANDRAL
          From a spring that I discovered, in
          which hydrogen sulfide is present.

                    ULYSSES
          Okay—

                    ANDRAL
          It may have curative properties for
          cancer!

                    ULYSSES
          What happened to Swamp-Root and
          bottled cures?

                    ANDRAL
          I sold the business to your uncle,
          and retired from that quest.

                    ULYSSES
          What?

Andral freezes, then suddenly weeps:

                    ANDRAL
          I'm heartbroken to let it go; my
          name is on the door. But the
          business grew too big for me—

Ulysses stares at his weakened father.

                    ULYSSES
          We'll make it right.

EXT. HELL'S KITCHEN - DAY

Willis walks along a street in Manhattan.

                    WILLIS
          Christ on the cross.

He sidesteps garbage on the sidewalk, surveying a derelict
neighborhood.

                    BOY
          Ya'made a wrong turn, dude!

Willis glares and picks up his pace.

EXT. 33RD STREET - DUSK

Willis walks down a busy block, through light rain, looking
for a drink and a place to rest.

INT. WALDORF HOTEL - NIGHT

Willis steps into the newly built Waldorf. He navigates its palatial Siena marble lobby — packed with clerks, elevator boys, and guests.

                    WILLIS
          Pardon me, sir!

A sturdy maître d' turns, and speaks in a thick Swiss accent:

                    OSCAR
          Hello young man, I am Oscar of the
          Waldorf. How may I help?

                    WILLIS
          I need a room. But first, *a drink—*

                    OSCAR
          Right this way.

INT. PALM ROOM - NIGHT

Willis and Oscar walk through a glass entrance to a restaurant. Willis looks up at stained glass, then to palm fronds around him. Oscar pulls out a chair.

                    OSCAR
          Please, have a seat—

Willis sits.

                    WILLIS
          What would you recommend?

                    OSCAR
          Where are you visiting from?

                    WILLIS
          Binghamton.

Oscar nods.

                    OSCAR
          A martini.

INT. PALM ROOM - NIGHT

Willis surveys the room for young women. Oscar returns with an elegant martini glass.

                    OSCAR
          Enjoy—

Willis sips at his table. He spots a stunningly attractive
blonde across the room and gets up to approach her.

INT. PALM ROOM - CONTINUOUS

                    WILLIS
          Excuse me—

The young woman looks up.

                    WILLIS (CONT'D)
          My name is Willis Sharpe Kilmer.
          May I ask yours?

                    BEATRICE
          Beatrice.

                    WILLIS
          Is it crazy for me to ask to join
          you?

                    BEATRICE
          Not crazy at all.

INT. PALM ROOM - NIGHT

Willis leans in.

                    WILLIS
          Where did you friends go?

                    BEATRICE
          To see a play—

                    WILLIS
          I'm in town researching advertising
          for my family business.

                    BEATRICE
          My father is an advertising agent.

Willis pauses.

                    WILLIS
          Fascinating. Can he help me?

                    BEATRICE
          I'm sure that he'd love to.

                         WILLIS
              Then I must see you again—

She smiles.

INT. OFFICE - DAY

Hadsell enters.

                         JONAS
              We won't make payroll today.

                         HADSELL
              What do we do?

                         JONAS
              We desperately need a loan.
              Nothing's wrong with our
              operations, but cash is drained
              after settling my brother's
              accounts.

                         HADSELL
              Why don't we go to City National
              Bank?

                         JONAS
              Because I'm a man of pride. I want
              to be our leading citizen, and
              can't allow them the satisfaction —
              give them the ammunition — of
              seeing me like this, begging them
              to save us. A few of their
              directors probably want me to fail—

                         HADSELL
              What about Rosefsky, the horse
              thief?

Jonas laughs.

                         JONAS
              Thanks for lightening my mood,
              Hadsell. How will a filthy wanderer
              help us?

                         HADSELL
              He has money to lend.

Jonas pauses.

                         JONAS
              Let's see him right away.

EXT. OSBORNE HOLLOW, NEW YORK - DAY

Andral stands alongside a creek and looks toward a small hill, then to dozens of men constructing a hotel.

                    ANDRAL
          I am investing the entirety of my
          Swamp-Root funds!

A small gathering of people claps in front of a completed spring house with a stone fountain inside.

                    SENATOR ROOT
          We thank you, Doctor Kilmer, for
          this brilliant sanitarium!

They cut a small ribbon with scissors.

                    ANDRAL
          We must rename this town *Sanitaria
          Springs.* Our Epidaurus—

The senator is baffled.

EXT. WEST 74TH STREET - DAY

Willis paces in front of a stone-trimmed townhouse, practicing his lines:

                    WILLIS
          Sir, what are your thoughts on the
          most effective form of advertising?

He thinks for a moment.

                    WILLIS (CONT'D)
          That's the key question.

EXT. WEST 74TH STREET - CONTINUOUS

Willis knocks on a door. It opens:

                    BEATRICE
          Isn't it lovely to see you—

She smiles and they embrace.

                    BEATRICE (CONT'D)
          Come inside!

INT. WEST 74TH STREET - DAY

Willis walks into a grand living room.

                    BEATRICE
          Please, meet my father—

                    WILLIS
          It's a pleasure, Mister Richardson.

Willis extends a hand.

                    MR. RICHARDSON
          So you're interested in
          advertising?

                    WILLIS
          To promote my family business, sir—

Willis and Beatrice sit on a couch next to each other; the
latter peels a banana.

                    MR. RICHARDSON
          What type of business?

                    WILLIS
          Health cures. My father bought it
          from my uncle, who is a doctor.

                    MR. RICHARDSON
          You mean *patent medicines?*

                    WILLIS
          Yes sir. What do you think is the
          most effective advertising?

                    MR. RICHARDSON
          Newspapers. I will place your ads
          in newspapers.

Willis raises his eyebrows, ecstatically.

                    WILLIS
          What will it cost me?

                    MR. RICHARDSON
          No money whatsoever.

                    WILLIS
          How can that be?

                    MR. RICHARDSON
          Because I want you to advise me on
          investing in my own patent
          medicines. I have visions of
          Ozomulsion, a cod liver tonic—

Willis stands up to shake his hand.

                    WILLIS
          Sir, you have yourself a deal!

INT. DR. KILMER & CO. - DAY

A line of indignant workers forms.

                    WORKER
          It's five o'clock; where's Kilmer
          with our paychecks?

                    EASLEY
          Hold your horses! He's on his way.

EXT. WEST 74TH STREET - DAY

Willis exits the townhouse, with Beatrice behind him.

                    BEATRICE
          When will I see you again?

                    WILLIS
          I'll be back soon, and as a richer
          man. Please give your father my
          thanks.

                    BEATRICE
          He clearly likes you.

                    WILLIS
          And I like you—

He kisses her lips.

INT. NINTH AVENUE ELEVATED RAILWAY - DAY

Willis thunders into Midtown.

INT. OFFICE - DAY

Jonas and Hadsell sit in Rosefsky's office.

                    ROSEFSKY
          Ten percent.

                    JONAS
          That's reasonable—

                    ROSEFSKY
          Monthly.

Jonas sits upright in his chair, as Hadsell grabs his leg.
They pause.

                    JONAS
          We have no choice.

                    ROSEFSKY
          Sign here—

Rosefsky slides a paper over the desk.

EXT. FIELD - DAY

Andral turns to Ulysses:

                    ANDRAL
          I hope that you'll spend time at
          the property as a superintendent.
          Our sulfur bath will be open at the
          end of summer—

                    ULYSSES
          Sulfur cures cancer?

                    ANDRAL
          Yes it does, and sanitariums will
          be our new business. We'll build
          more hydrotherapiums and
          cancertoriums as well—

                    ULYSSES
          What are *those?*

                    ANDRAL
          They provide treatments for
          patients, who will rent rooms and
          buy services, much like hotels.

INT. DR. KILMER & CO. - DAY

Jonas and Hadsell burst through the door.

                    WORKER
          Are we going to get paid? We got
          families to feed!

                    JONAS
          Gentlemen, we're here with your
          cash!

Jonas opens an envelope stuffed with dollars, and begins
disbursing pay.

INT. HOME - DUSK

Jonas pushes open his front door. He walks into his living
room and collapses onto the couch.

                                        FADE TO BLACK.

EXT. TRAIN STATION - DAY

Willis alights and strolls toward Chenango Street. He puffs
from a cigar.

INT. ARLINGTON HOTEL - DAY

Ulysses sits at a bar and slams down whiskey.

EXT. ARLINGTON HOTEL - DAY

Willis turns to enter the Arlington and, suddenly, is face to
face with a drunken Ulysses.

                    ULYSSES
          Hello, cousin.

                    WILLIS
          Hello, Ula—

                    ULYSSES
          How is Swamp-Root doing?

                    WILLIS
          We're workin' hard—

                    ULYSSES
          You stole it!

                    WILLIS
          Whoa, calm down!

Ulysses shoves him.

                    ULYSSES
          You're a swindler, and don't know
          anything about medicine!

He throws a punch and misses.

                    WILLIS
          Son of a bitch.

Willis puts him in a chokehold, as others rush to break up
the altercation.

                    ULYSSES
          Swindlers!

Willis grips his throat tighter; Ulysses retches.

                                        DISSOLVE TO:

INT. POLICE DEPARTMENT - DAY

Jonas approaches and shakes hands with a police chief.

                    CHIEF
          We're thankful to have you as a
          police commissioner.

                    JONAS
          We'll keep Binghamton great.

                    CHIEF
          Did you see the attacks against
          Mayor Green in the newspaper?

                    JONAS
          No—

The chief whistles.

                    CHIEF
          The Herald is vicious.

INT. DR. KILMER & CO. - DAY

Willis sits at a table, dominant, with a crisp black suit on.

                    WILLIS
          Our new advertising campaign is
          running.

                    HADSELL
          You won't believe it—

Jonas walks in.

                    HADSELL (CONT'D)
          We're on track to sell ten times as
          much as last week.

                                        CUT TO:

EXT. NEWSPAPER STAND, PHILADELPHIA - DAY

"ARE YOUR KIDNEYS WEAK?" "Thousands of Women Have Kidney
Trouble and Never Suspect It!"

INT. DRUGSTORE, MANHATTAN - DAY

A trade card showing children examining a framed image of
crocodiles: "Use Dr. Kilmer's," "Swamp-Root," "Kidney, Liver
& Bladder Cure."

INT. DRUGSTORE, MANHATTAN - CONTINUOUS

                    CUSTOMER
          Swamp-Root, please.

                    DRUGGIST
          One large bottle?

                    CUSTOMER
          Make it two—

INT. MAGAZINE AISLE - DAY

"CURED BY SWAMP-ROOT." "Sample Bottle Sent Absolutely Free by
Mail." "Dr. Kilmer & Co., Binghamton, N.Y."

INT. KITCHEN - DAY

A man pours Swamp-Root from a bottle into a glass and gulps
it down.

                                        DISSOLVE TO:

INT. DR. KILMER & CO. - DAY

Willis works on an assembly line packing bottles.

> HADSELL
> Can you believe this?

> WILLIS
> *The power of advertising.*

> HADSELL
> I'm working late tonight with your
> father—

> WILLIS
> How many crates have we packed?

> HADSELL
> Nearly five thousand of Swamp-Root.

> WILLIS
> Two dozen bottles per crate. Buck a
> bottle. *For the love of God—*

> HADSELL
> Over a hundred grand.

EXT. CARRIAGE HOUSE, SANITARIA SPRINGS - DUSK

Light flickers within a house that straddles Osborne Creek.

INT. CARRIAGE HOUSE, SANITARIA SPRINGS - NIGHT

Andral sits at a desk across from a brick fireplace with a
crackling blaze. He reads from a stack of newspapers.

> ANDRAL
> Cancer treatment—

He rifles through pages and rips out articles:

> ANDRAL (CONT'D)
> *Can cancer be cured?*

Andral tears out another article. He reaches for a scrapbook
and writes on its cover: Dr. S. Andral Kilmer & Co.

> ANDRAL (CONT'D)
> Save these—

Manically, he cuts out more articles with scissors, affixing
them into his scrapbook.

> FADE TO BLACK.

EXT. 65TH STREET TRANSVERSE - DAY

Willis crosses Central Park in a carriage, confident and debonair.

                    WILLIS
          Pick up the pace, I don't want to
          be late!

                    COACHMAN
          Hup, hup!

                    WILLIS
          Whip anybody who gets in our way!

The coachman rolls his eyes.

EXT. WEST 74TH STREET - DAY

Willis knocks on a door. It opens:

                    MR. RICHARDSON
          The Sultan of Swamp-Root!

Willis grins.

                    WILLIS
          I can't thank you enough, Mister
          Richardson—

                    MR. RICHARDSON
          Come on in.

INT. TOWNHOUSE - DAY

They walk into the living room.

                    MR. RICHARDSON
          I'm astounded by how effective your
          advertising is. You're up there
          with Paine's Celery Compound or,
          dare I say, Lydia E. Pinkham
          herself, the queen of quackery!

Willis laughs.

                    WILLIS
          Our sales have exploded—

                    MR. RICHARDSON
          We kicked off a bull market in
          patent medicines.

INT. TOWNHOUSE - CONTINUOUS

                    MR. RICHARDSON
          Beatrice! Willis is here—

He turns to Willis:

                    MR. RICHARDSON (CONT'D)
          Have fun shopping.

EXT. UNION SQUARE - DAY

Willis and Beatrice saunter along Union Square.

EXT. TIFFANY & CO. - DAY

The couple stands beneath a magisterial cast-iron building.

                    WILLIS
          Shall we go in?

Beatrice blushes.

INT. TIFFANY & CO. - DAY

Willis and Beatrice walk through a palace of jewels.

                    BEATRICE
          Oh my—

They look at a display case filled with sterling silver
kitchenware.

                    WILLIS
          Let's buy a little something.

She is surprised, and impressed.

INT. TIFFANY & CO. - CONTINUOUS

Willis surveys a well-heeled clientele, as a salesman stands
across the counter:

                    SALESMAN
          Anything catch your eye?

                    WILLIS
          Everything does—

They smile.

                    SALESMAN
          How about a sterling silver
          butterfly brooch for this lovely
          young lady?

He takes a piece from under glass and slides it across the
counter.

                    BEATRICE
          Why thank you—

She fastens it to her lapel, and turns to Willis:

                    BEATRICE (CONT'D)
          How do I look?

                    WILLIS
          Beautiful. But we need to complete
          it. Let's see this—

                    SALESMAN
          The platinum solitaire engagement
          ring?

                    WILLIS
          Please.

                    BEATRICE
          You can't be serious—

                    WILLIS
          Try it on.

Willis takes the ring and slides it onto her finger.

                    WILLIS (CONT'D)
               (softly)
          Will you?

Her eyes open wide.

                                        DISSOLVE TO:

INT. SANITARIUM - DAY

Andral greets elderly women at the sanitarium.

                    ANDRAL
          Welcome! You're the first patients
          to receive treatment at my cutting-
          edge facility. You shall experience
          the best that modern medicine
          offers—

EXT. SANITARIUM - DAY

Ulysses stands at the edge of the woods holding a potted
plant. Andral speaks to a group of women sitting under a
gazebo, as Ulysses hands out leaves.

                    ANDRAL
          Here is the Indian Red Iron Spring,
          from which your cancer will be
          cured, assisted by cooling forest
          leaves.

A dog barks.

INT. SANITARIUM - DUSK

Ulysses holds up an advertisement.

                    ULYSSES
          Can you believe they're still
          advertising Swamp-Root with *your*
          name and face?

Andral turns:

                    ANDRAL
          Let it go.

                                        DISSOLVE TO:

INT. FIFTH AVENUE HOTEL - MORNING

Willis adjusts a cravat.

                    CYRUS
          Solemnly, may we gather for your
          funeral—

Willis smirks.

                    WILLIS
          At least I get to smell the orange
          blossoms.

                    CYRUS
          Will there be other ladies in
          attendance?

                    WILLIS
          Get this: Anna Gould, the Countess
          de Castellane.

                    CYRUS
          Jay Gould's daughter?

                    WILLIS
          She ain't good looking, and her new
          husband, the Count, is rippin'
          through her inheritance like
          wildfire. He loves men, too—

                    CYRUS
          You're saying that I may have a
          chance with the Count?

Willis laughs.

EXT. WEST 74TH STREET - DAY

Willis and Cyrus stand outside the Richardsons' home.

                    WILLIS
               Show time.

They walk up the steps.

INT. TOWNHOUSE - DAY

A man plays piano across from mahogany panels and a crackling
fire. The room is filled with roses and maidenhair ferns. The
maid of honor, with pink roses, proceeds in a pale blue
dress. Willis stares at her face.

                                        FLASHBACK TO:

EXT. PARK - DUSK

Willis is face to face with a girl.

                    ANNA
          Where are you going with those bone-
          shakers?

                    RAWLINGS
          To the Navy Yard!

                                        DISSOLVE TO:

INT. TOWNHOUSE - DAY

Willis, gulping, continues to stare. He feels a fight-or-flight rush.

                                        FLASHBACK TO:

EXT. PARK - DUSK

                    ANNA
          What are those pants?

She points.

                    ANNA (CONT'D)
          They look so tight. Are you a girl,
          too?

Laughter erupts.

                                        DISSOLVE TO:

INT. TOWNHOUSE - DAY

Beatrice, on her father's arm, wears a white satin gown adorned with pearls and orange blossoms, with a sweeping court train. Her father lifts a tulle veil — fastened with a diamond tiara — from her golden hair.

INT. TOWNHOUSE - CONTINUOUS

Beatrice looks to her imminent husband's distant gaze.

INT. TOWNHOUSE - CONTINUOUS

A faint scent of coal smoke and lilies hangs in the air.

                    REVEREND TOWNSEND
          The ring—

Cyrus steps forth and produces a ring, setting it on the minister's open palm.

                    REVEREND TOWNSEND (CONT'D)
          Bless this ring, that he who gives
          it, and she who wears it, may abide
          in peace unto their life's end,
          through Jesus Christ our Lord.

                    WILLIS
          Amen.

                                        CUT TO BLACK.

EXT. RIVERSIDE DRIVE, BINGHAMTON - MORNING

Damp sod slopes down to a slow Susquehanna.

EXT. RIVERSIDE DRIVE - CONTINUOUS

Workers tramp through mud.

EXT. RIVERSIDE DRIVE - CONTINUOUS

Workers clear trees, as Jonas points:

                    JONAS
          This plot. A perfect view—

                    VOSBURY
          What do you envision?

                    JONAS
          Mansions far grander than what's
          next door.

They look to the Rose mansion.

                    VOSBURY
          Mansions, plural?

                    JONAS
          My son Willis needs one, too.
          Everything we do is side by side—

                    VOSBURY
          How about my sketch inspired by a
          castle?

                    JONAS
          We'll start there! I have a million
          dollars. I want to live like a
          Vanderbilt.

EXT. RIVERSIDE DRIVE - DAY

Stonemasons lay a foundation.

                                        DISSOLVE TO:

INT. SANITARIUM - DAY

Ulysses enters.

                    ANDRAL
          The sanitarium is glorious—

                    ULYSSES
          Dad, be proud of all that you have
          accomplished.

                    ANDRAL
          Yet I'm almost out of cash.

                    ULYSSES
          Huh?

                    ANDRAL
          Our facilities absorbed it all.

                    ULYSSES
          What should we do?

                    ANDRAL
          We'll wait it out.

EXT. KILMER MANSION - DAY

Stonework on a turret is complete, as workers roam the site.

                    JONAS
          I'm grateful that my son became
          friends with you!

Cyrus, in work clothes, laughs.

                    CYRUS
          I appreciate it, Mister Kilmer.

                    JONAS
          Your men are doing a beautiful job—

                    CYRUS
          We'll be done with your stonework
          right on schedule.

EXT. TRAIN STATION - DAY

Willis and Beatrice arrive in Binghamton.

                    WILLIS
          I wish that we could stay in
          Manhattan, but my business is here.

                    BEATRICE
          This is your home.

INT. BANK - DAY

Andral stands at a bank counter.

                    MANAGER
          Your account is overdrawn.

                    ANDRAL
          What does that mean?

                    MANAGER
          You have no money left, and your
          balance is negative.

                    ANDRAL
          What can we do? I have nothing else
          to fill that hole, or pay my other
          bills—

                    MANAGER
          I will connect you with our
          attorney to prepare a bankruptcy
          filing.

EXT. KILMER MANSION - DUSK

Ulysses stands on Riverside Drive staring at Jonas's mansion.
It is illuminated and guests roam through elegant rooms.

                    ULYSSES
          I can't believe my own eyes.

His gaze burns with resentment.

                    ULYSSES (CONT'D)
                (under his breath)
            Swindlers!

INT. KILMER MANSION - NIGHT

A toast:

                    MR. DAVIDGE
          To the man who has it all. Jonas
          Kilmer, the baron of our time!

Jonas laughs as guests cheer and raise their glasses.

                                        DISSOLVE TO:

EXT. DR. KILMER & CO. - NIGHT

The street is silent. Kilmer's factory kindles.

INT. KILMER MANSION - NIGHT

Willis and Beatrice drink and celebrate.

EXT. DR. KILMER & CO. - NIGHT

Suddenly, the facility is consumed by a conflagration.

INT. KILMER MANSION - NIGHT

Hadsell approaches Jonas, surrounded by guests, with a
stricken face.

                    HADSELL
          Sir—

Jonas motions him to back away.

                    JONAS
          Please, Hadsell, this is my night
          to indulge!

                    HADSELL
          Sir, you need to get in your
          carriage right away.

INT./EXT. CARRIAGE - NIGHT

Jonas and Willis bound through Binghamton. They ride in
silence beneath the glow of streetlamps, shadows dancing
across their faces.

EXT. DR. KILMER & CO. - NIGHT

Jonas steps out of his carriage, stunned.

                    JONAS
          Lord have mercy—

He stares at his factory, engulfed in flames. Willis stands
behind him.

                    JONAS (CONT'D)
          Everything we have—

Slowly, softly, as a tear runs down his face:

                    JONAS (CONT'D)
          Gone.

A wall collapses into the inferno.

                                        FADE TO BLACK.

                                        FADE IN:

EXT. DELAWARE PARK LAKE, BUFFALO - DAWN

A mighty white oak sways in the wind.

EXT. TEMPLE OF MUSIC - DAY

A large crowd gathers for the Pan-American Exposition.

EXT. TRIUMPHAL BRIDGE - DAY

A procession marches in lockstep for the fair's opening.

                    ANDRAL
          Do you see Theodore Roosevelt?

Ulysses scans men in military uniforms.

                    ULYSSES
          There he is!

The Vice President walks by and waves.

INT. FINE ARTS GALLERY - DAY

Andral and Ulysses approach a painting of the Adirondacks
near Lake Placid by James Craig Nicoll.

                    ULYSSES
          Will we see President McKinley as
          well?

                    ANDRAL
          He won't visit the Pan-American
          Exposition until after we leave.

                                        DISSOLVE TO:

EXT. BINGHAMTON GLASS CO. - NIGHT

Summer, 1900. Streets are still; signs for bottling hang on
factory's front. Suddenly, it bursts into flames.

                                        CUT TO:

EXT. ELECTRIC TOWER - DUSK

Ulysses and his father stand beneath a magnificent tower;
water gushing from its face like Niagara.

                    ULYSSES
          Let's see the top of the Electric
          Tower!

Andral raises an eyebrow. Crowds of men in bowlers and women
in fitted bodices pass behind them.

                                        FLASHBACK TO:

EXT. STREET - DAY

Willis vaingloriously guides a tandem carriage. Traffic fills
the streets. A wobbly bicyclist weaves in front of him.

                                        CUT TO:

INT. UPPER LANDING - DUSK

An elevator door opens, and Ulysses and Andral step out.

                    ANDRAL
          Stunning—

They stare across the Court of Fountains, taking in a vista
overlooking the Exposition and Buffalo.

                                        FLASHBACK TO:

EXT. STREET - DAY

Willis shouts:

                         WILLIS
                   Get out of the way!

The bicyclist, deaf to Willis's words, continues veering
toward his carriage.

                         WILLIS (CONT'D)
                   Damn it, get out of my way!

Willis cracks his horsewhip across the bicyclist's back.

                                             CUT TO:

INT. UPPER LANDING - NIGHT

Suddenly, beneath a statue of the Goddess of Light at the
tower's top, pale green spotlights shoot out. Lights flip on
across the fair, illuminating buildings and fountains.

                         ANDRAL
                   It's a new age.

The crowd is ecstatic.

                                             DISSOLVE TO:

EXT. BEMAN & COMPANY BARREL FACTORY - NIGHT

A wooden packaging company, with Swamp-Root boxes stacked up,
swiftly ignites.

                                             CUT TO BLACK.

EXT. TRAIN STATION - DAY

Andral walks from a train after arriving in Binghamton.

INT. WILLIS'S MANSION - MORNING

Willis weaves through a hardwood-paneled hallway of his new
home.

                         WILLIS
                   Beatrice!

INT. SOUTH STREET FACTORY - DAY

Jonas sits at a makeshift desk as Andral enters.

                    ANDRAL
          How much do I owe you?

                    JONAS
          Nothing.

                    ANDRAL
          Nothing for bailing out my
          sanitarium?

Jonas holds up a statement showing a sum of $14,255.58 and
tears it in half.

                    JONAS
          Nothing! I'm proud to be in a
          position to extinguish your debts.

                    ANDRAL
          I can't thank you enough—

He puts his hand on Jonas's.

                    ANDRAL (CONT'D)
          Especially after your setback with
          the fire.

Jonas pauses.

                    JONAS
          Our supply was razed, but the
          demand wasn't. We're already back
          on track.

Jonas stands and motions toward a shop floor, teeming with
workers.

                    ANDRAL
          Brother, we still have everything
          to be proud of.

They embrace.

EXT. BEMAN & COMPANY BARREL FACTORY - NIGHT

Beman's Frederick Street storehouse is a burned husk. The
facility explodes into flames again. Elbert Beman rushes to
the street:

                    BEMAN
          What the hell is happening! *What
          the hell is happening!*

                                        DISSOLVE TO:

INT./EXT. WILLIS'S MANSION - DAY

Willis steps out onto a stately stone porch.

                    BEATRICE
          Join me for a drink, love—

Willis pulls out a chair, next to a resting bull terrier.

INT. POLICE DEPARTMENT - DAY

Jonas strides down a hallway, his heels clacking on tile.

                    JONAS
          What the hell is happening?

                    CHIEF
          Commissioner Kilmer, our detectives
          identified a culprit and are
          planning an arrest.

                    JONAS
          My factory, my bottle supplier, my
          box supplier — am I crazy? Crazy to
          think that this is a conspiracy to
          cripple my business?

                    CHIEF
          I can't speak to his motive, sir.
          But your arsonist is a man named
          Slater. Arthur Slater.

                    JONAS
          Never heard of him. Who is he?

                    CHIEF
          Janitor at Beman's barrel factory.
          He's either insane or got a
          vendetta against Beman. But he
          wasn't targeting you. Beman hired
          night watchmen and a private
          detective; we're workin' with them
          to build a case and bring Slater to
          justice.

EXT. WILLIS'S MANSION - DAY

Willis sips from a beer bottle.

                    BEATRICE
          I'm not happy here.

                    WILLIS
          What do you want, a vacation?

                    BEATRICE
          I want you to keep your eyes and
          hands off of other women, to start.
          And Florida would be nice—

He is taken off guard.

                    WILLIS
          What are you talking about?

                    BEATRICE
          I'm not a fool, Willis.

                    WILLIS
          Not a fool, okay; but what do you
          do around this house? Did you make
          dinner *once* since we moved in? Do
          you do *anything* for me! You sit
          here with your stupid dog all day—

                    BEATRICE
          Go to hell.

In a flash of fury, Willis whips a half-full beer bottle at
her face and she screams.

                              DISSOLVE TO:

INT. BEMAN & COMPANY BARREL FACTORY - DUSK

Elbert Beman shuts down his factory for the night.

                    BEMAN
          You'll be the watchman tonight?

                    SLATER
          Yes, Mister Beman.

                    BEMAN
          I appreciate it, Slater. I'm going
          to sleep.

Beman walks to the door, then peers back suspiciously.

EXT. BEMAN & COMPANY BARREL FACTORY - NIGHT

Beman meets a private detective as he steps outside.

                    BEMAN
          I don't trust him an inch.

                    HASTINGS
          I'll keep an eye on him through the
          window.

                    BEMAN
          I'll stay with you. I'm not going
          home tonight.

EXT. LOCKWOOD ESTATE - DAY

Willis stands on Lewis Street near the railroad station.

                    WILLIS
          I'll buy everything.

                    LOCKWOOD
          My entire estate?

They scan land and a wood home.

                    WILLIS
          Yeah, everything.

EXT./INT. BEMAN & COMPANY BARREL FACTORY - NIGHT

Beman and Hastings peer through a window.

                    BEMAN
          I don't see him.

They surveil the factory.

                    HASTINGS
          Look there—

                    BEMAN
          What's he doing?

                    HASTINGS
          Gathering rags.

Slater pulls out a bucket and looks around to be sure that he
is alone. He fills it with rags.

                    HASTINGS (CONT'D)
          Here we go.

                    BEMAN
          What?

Slater pours fuel into the bucket.

                    HASTINGS
          Kerosene. There's your man—

                    BEMAN
          Let's get him!

Slater shoves the bucket under a bench and scurries away.

EXT. BEMAN & COMPANY BARREL FACTORY - NIGHT

Beman and Hastings rush to find Slater. They crouch behind a
bush, spotting him opening a door.

                    BEMAN
          What's he doing?

                    HASTINGS
          Quiet—

EXT. BEMAN & COMPANY BARREL FACTORY - CONTINUOUS

They observe Slater meeting with a mysterious figure who
speaks in a muffled voice.

                    SLATER
          How much tonight?

                    SHADOWY MAN
          One hundred.

                    SLATER
          You said up to a thousand!

                    SHADOWY MAN
          I only have a hundred right now.

                    SLATER
          Give it—

A fistful of bills changes hands.

EXT. BEMAN & COMPANY BARREL FACTORY - CONTINUOUS

Hastings observes this exchange.

                    HASTINGS
          Fascinating.

                         BEMAN
               What the hell is going on?

EXT. BEMAN & COMPANY BARREL FACTORY - CONTINUOUS

Other men are visible.

                       SHADOWY MAN
               We will make a sure thing of it
               this time.

Slater turns to go back inside, while others depart for the
street. As the dark conspirator moves into moonlight, his
face is revealed — Ulysses Kilmer.

EXT. FREDERICK STREET - NIGHT

Ulysses strikes a match, raises it, and sucks on a cigarette.
He tosses the match and exhales. Nonchalantly:

                        ULYSSES
               Swindlers.

                                        CUT TO BLACK.

EXT. LOCKWOOD ESTATE - MORNING

Lockwood's house is dismantled by workers, as they clear the
property.

EXT. LOCKWOOD ESTATE - DAY

Willis, Cyrus, and Jonas observe a construction site with
steel beams stacked and waiting.

                         CYRUS
               Riveted steel. Your new building
               will be entirely fireproof — still
               standing centuries from now.

                        WILLIS
               What do you think about being right
               next to the tracks?

Jonas turns:

                        JONAS
               I think it makes clear who runs
               this town.

EXT. LACKAWANNA RAILROAD STATION - DAY

Beatrice stands alone with her bags and a black eye.

INT. BROOME COUNTY JAIL - DAY

A door opens and Ulysses is escorted into a cell by police
officers.

                    SHERIFF
          Make yourself at home.

Ulysses sits on a bed.

                    ULYSSES
          Two packs of cigarettes, please.

The sheriff scoffs and slams shut the cell door.

EXT. WASHINGTON STREET - DAY

Willis angrily marches through downtown with a newspaper in
his hand.

INT. BINGHAMTON EVENING HERALD - DAY

Willis storms into a red brick building.

                    WILLIS
          I need to speak with the
          newspaper's editor!

                    SECRETARY
          The office to the left, sir—

INT. BINGHAMTON EVENING HERALD - CONTINUOUS

Willis enters the editor's office.

                    BEARDSLEY
          Hello there! Guy Beardsley, the
          Herald's owner and editor. How may
          I help?

He extends a hand. It hangs there.

                    WILLIS
          How the hell do you explain this?

Beardsley retracts and raises his eyebrows.

                    WILLIS (CONT'D)
          Why did you print this about me
          whipping that cyclist?

                    BEARDSLEY
          Because it was and is a matter of
          court procedure.

                    WILLIS
          Why didn't you come to me?

                    BEARDSLEY
          What do you mean?

                    WILLIS
          I mean that I would have made it
          right with you. I would have made
          it worth something to you to keep
          it out—

                    BEARDSLEY
          A bribe? Mister Kilmer, we're a
          principled publication.

Willis's face turns red.

                    WILLIS
          Then you can forget about the Swamp-
          Root advertising that we have in
          your pages!

Beardsley is taken aback.

                    WILLIS (CONT'D)
          I should horsewhip *you!*

Willis exits, slamming the door behind him.

                                        DISSOLVE TO:

INT. BROOME COUNTY JAIL - DAY

Ulysses' cell opens. Jonas enters, as a door clangs shut
behind him.

                    JONAS
          I should slap your face.

He pauses.

                    JONAS (CONT'D)
          I should slap you right to the
          ground!

Another pause.

                    JONAS (CONT'D)
          Lock you behind bars for a decade.
          And you know damn well that I have
          the power to do so.

A tear rolls down Ulysses' cheek.

                    JONAS (CONT'D)
          But I won't.

Ulysses looks up.

                    ULYSSES
          My father knows nothing about this.

                    JONAS
          I don't know what the hell you were
          thinking. I don't want to know. But
          we'll put this behind us — our
          family — right now. Square deal?

                    ULYSSES
          Yes, sir.

                                        DISSOLVE TO:

EXT. BROOME COUNTY JAIL - DAY

Ulysses walks out alone, his head hung down.

EXT. INDIAN MOUND, SANITARIA SPRINGS - DAY

www.ingramcontent.com/pod-product-compliance
Lightning Source LLC
Chambersburg PA
CBHW081916120726

47996CB00010B/3348